Illustrated by Tommy Stubbs

 A GOLDEN BOOK • NEW YORK

Thomas the Tank Engine & Friends™

CREATED BY BRITT ALLCROFT

Based on the Railway Series by the Reverend W Awdry.
© 2016 Gullane (Thomas) LLC. Thomas the Tank Engine & Friends and Thomas & Friends are trademarks of Gullane (Thomas) Limited. Thomas the Tank Engine & Friends and Design Is Reg. U.S. Pat. & Tm. Off. © 2016 HIT Entertainment Limited. All rights reserved. Published in the United States by Golden Books, an imprint of Random House Children's Books, a division of Penguin Random House LLC, 1745 Broadway, New York, NY 10019, and in Canada by Penguin Random House Canada Limited, Toronto. Golden Books, A Golden Book, A Little Golden Book, the G colophon, and the distinctive gold spine are registered trademarks of Penguin Random House LLC.
ISBN 978-1-101-93756-3 (trade) — ISBN 978-1-101-93757-0 (ebook)
randomhousekids.com
www.thomasandfriends.com
Printed in the United States of America
10 9 8 7 6 5 4 3
Random House Children's Books supports the First Amendment and celebrates the right to read.

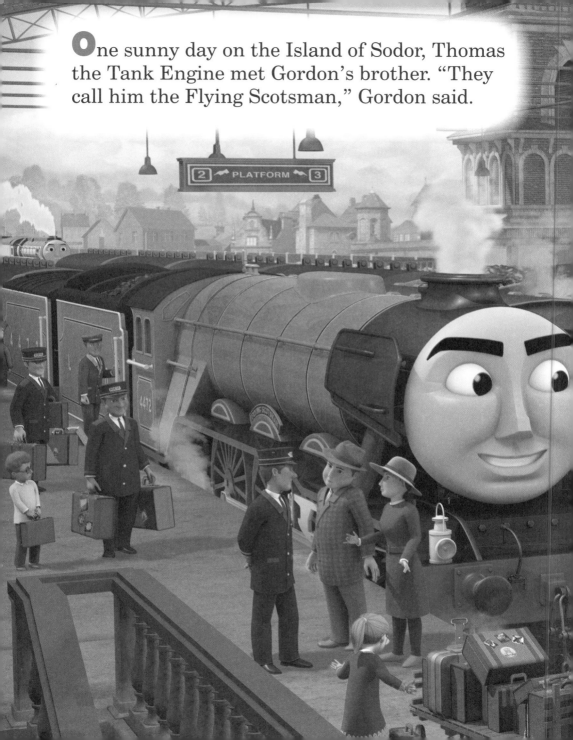

One sunny day on the Island of Sodor, Thomas the Tank Engine met Gordon's brother. "They call him the Flying Scotsman," Gordon said.

Gordon's brother was going to the Great Railway Show on the Mainland. "That's where engines compete to see who's the fastest and strongest," he explained.

Thomas really wanted to go, too.

Thomas asked Sir Topham Hatt about streamlining an engine from Sodor so it could compete—and win—at the show.

Sir Topham Hatt loved the idea. "We'll streamline Gordon to make him faster than ever."

Gordon was *not* the engine Thomas had in mind!

The next day, engines from all over the world arrived on Sodor.

"Where are you going?" the Dock Manager asked.

"The Great Railway Show," puffed one engine.

"That'll be on the Mainland," the Manager replied.

The engines hurried back onto the ferry.

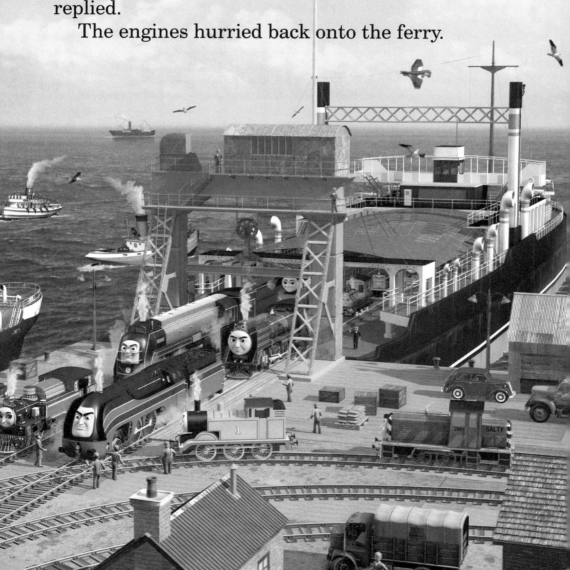

In her rush, a brightly painted engine named Ashima bumped into Thomas.

"Whoa!" he peeped as he teetered over the water.

Together the Dockworkers and Ashima pulled Thomas back from danger.

Ashima apologized and asked how she might get to the Mainland.

Thomas chugged away without answering.

"Why should *she* go to the Great Railway Show?"
Thomas puffed to his carriages.
"She *is* beautifully painted," Clarabel said.
"Any engine can get painted," Thomas puffed.
And that gave Thomas another idea.

At the Steamworks, Thomas asked Victor to repaint him. "I was thinking maybe lightning bolts and racing stripes," he said.

When Sir Topham Hatt stopped by to check on Gordon's streamlining, he liked the idea—but not for Thomas.

Over at the Dieselworks, Diesel had an idea of his own: to disguise a few diesels as his trucks and pretend to pull them.

"It will look like I'm pulling a very heavy train," he said with a snicker. "Sir Topham Hatt will think I'm stronger than Henry. He'll take *me* to the Great Railway Show."

Later that day, Thomas saw Ashima. She didn't understand why Thomas wanted to be repainted.

"You can only be you," she said. "Every engine is useful and has a job to do." Ashima asked Thomas if he was good at shunting and sorting trucks.

That gave Thomas his best idea yet. "I'll show Sir Topham Hatt what *I* can do best!"

The next day, Thomas went to Knapford Station to practice shunting. The rails were blocked by Diesel's tricky trucks, so Thomas started to move them.

"Hey! You'll spoil my trick!" Diesel hissed.

The disguised diesels began to chug along with Thomas. They moved quickly and easily!

At a red signal, Thomas tried to stop, but the diesels kept pushing.
CRASH! Thomas collided with another engine!

On the day of the Great Railway Show, the Sodor engines were ready to go. Gordon had been painted and streamlined. His new nameplate said The Shooting Star.

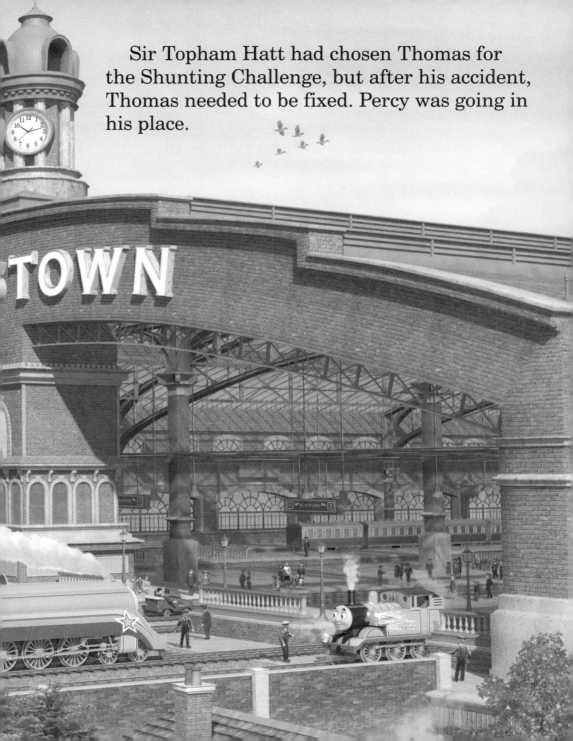

Sir Topham Hatt had chosen Thomas for the Shunting Challenge, but after his accident, Thomas needed to be fixed. Percy was going in his place.

Later, Victor realized that Gordon's safety valve hadn't been reinstalled after his streamlining. Without it, he could overheat!

Thomas rushed the valve to the Great Railway Show. But Gordon didn't believe him. And the race was starting!

Green flags waved and the engines took off!

Gordon raced along. Suddenly his face turned red. Steam hissed from inside his streamlining.

Gordon's brother told him something was wrong, but Gordon wouldn't listen. Then his boiler burst! He sputtered to a stop in a cloud of steam. The other engines sped on.

Meanwhile, over at the Shunting Challenge, Percy was scared. He asked Thomas to enter the race in his place. Thomas agreed. "I might lose, you know," he said.

But Thomas chuffed through round after
round, pulling tankers and flatbeds into line.
He beat big engines from many countries.

In the end, only Thomas and Ashima were left.
And then the final challenge began.

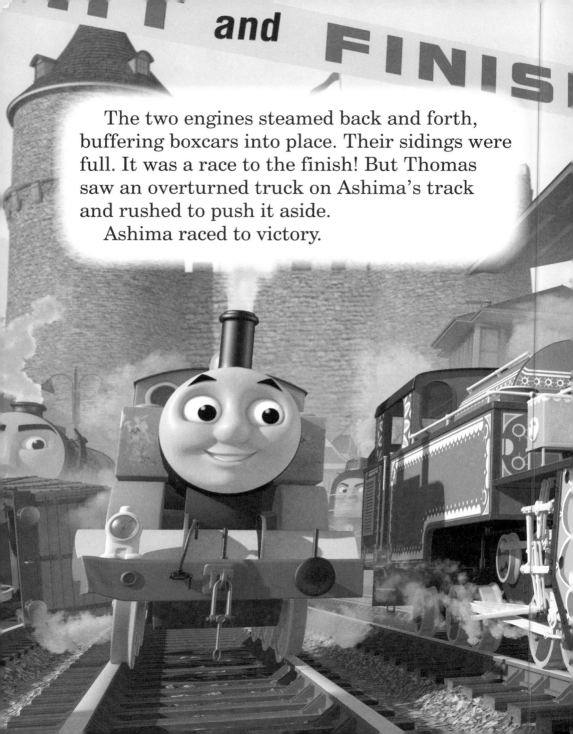

The two engines steamed back and forth, buffering boxcars into place. Their sidings were full. It was a race to the finish! But Thomas saw an overturned truck on Ashima's track and rushed to push it aside.

Ashima raced to victory.

At the award ceremony the judges had a surprise. "We would like to declare *two* winners in the Shunting Challenge. Ashima wins for being fastest. Thomas wins for helping his competitor!"

The engines whistled and cheered. They were all so impressed with the engines from Sodor.

Sir Topham Hatt was very proud of Thomas for being Really Useful—and a truly good sport.

"He was just being Thomas, Sir," Percy peeped.

"You can only be you," Thomas said, and winked at Ashima. "There's nothing else you can possibly do!"